I'm *Geronimo Stilton*'s sister. As I'm sure you know from my brother's bestselling novels, I'm a special correspondent for *The Rodent's Gazette*, Mouse Island's most famous newspaper. Unlike my 'fraidy mouse brother, I absolutely adore traveling, having adventures, and meeting rodents from all around the world!

The adventure I want to tell you about begins at Mouseford Academy, the school I went to when I was a young mouseling. I had such a great experience there as a student that I came back to teach a journalism class.

When I returned as a grown mouse, I met five really special students: Colette, Nicky, Pamela, Paulina, and Violet. You could hardly imagine five more different mouselings, but they became great friends right away. And they liked me so much that they decided to name their group after me: the Thea Sisters! I was so touched by that, I decided to write about their adventures. So turn the page to read a fabumouse adventure about the

THEA SISTERS!

Colette

She has a passion for clothing and style, especially anything pink. When she grows up, she wants to be a fashion editor.

Paulina

Cheerful and kind, she loves traveling and meeting rodents from all over the world. She has a magic touch when it comes to technology.

Violet

She's the bookworm of the group, and she loves learning. She enjoys classical music and dreams of becoming a famouse violinist.

THE THEA SISTERS

Nicky

She comes from Australia and is very enthusiastic about sports and nature. She loves being outside and is always ready to get up and go!

Pamela

She is a great mechanic: Give her a screwdriver and she'll fix anything! She loves pizza, which she eats every day, and she loves to cook.

Do you want to help the Thea Sisters in this new adventure? It's not hard — just follow the clues!

When you see this magnifying glass, pay attention: It means there's an important clue on the page. Each time one appears, we'll review the clues so we don't miss anything.

**ARE YOU READY?
A NEW MYSTERY AWAITS!**

Geronimo Stilton

Thea Stilton
AND THE
TROPICAL TREASURE

Scholastic Inc.

Text by Thea Stilton
Original title *Avventura ai Caraibi*
Cover by Barbara Pellizzari (design) and Flavio Ferron (color)
Illustrations by Barbara Pellizzari and Chiara Balleello (design), and Valeria Cairoli and Daniele Verzini (color)
Opening pages illustrations by Barbara Pellizzari (design) and Flavio Ferron (color)
Graphics by Elena Dal Maso

Special thanks to Beth Dunfey
Translated by Emily Clement
Interior design by Kay Petronio

10 9 8 7   17 18 19

Printed in the U.S.A.   40
First printing 2015

A SURPRISE VACATION

It was **morning** at Mouseford Academy, and Paulina woke with a big *smile* on her snout. For the first time in months, she had no classes to scurry off to and she could enjoy a little *relaxation* time. She decided to go to the computer lab to write an e-mail to her little sister, Maria, back in Peru.

When Paulina returned to her **ROOM**, she noticed something strange. She was sure she'd left everything neat and **tidy**, but now there were pens and notebooks all over her desk. Her **DATE BOOK** lay open to the current week — the beginning of their spring break. Someone had circled a date later in the week and **sketched** a sailboat there!

Beneath the sketch was a *note* that said, *See you at noon in the cafeteria.*

"**NOON?**" Paulina said, checking her watch. "That's in five minutes!"

She **SCAMPERED** out of her room and almost smacked into Pam, who was *RACING* down the hallway.

"Hey, Paulina, **LOOK** where you're going!" Pam said.

"Hi there. What are you eating?" Paulina asked her friend, who was always nibbling on something.

"Someone **LEFT** these in my room," Pam replied, holding up a little bag of gummies shaped like palm trees. "With a note that said . . ."

"To go to the cafeteria at noon!" finished Colette, joining her friends. "I found the same **message** in my locker,

along with this." She pulled out a cute stuffed flamingo.

"But why? **What's** going on?" asked Paulina.

"Let's find out!" Pam replied.

In the **CAFETERIA**, they found Violet examining a large map. She was so **absorbed** she didn't notice her friends until they were practically stepping on her tail.

"Vi, did you ask us to *come* here?" asked Colette, sitting down next to her.

Violet shook her snout. "**Nope.** I found this map of the Caribbean in my room, along with a *note* telling me to meet here at noon."

"A map of the Caribbean? Cool!" Pam said.

"A sailboat, palm trees, a flamingo, a map of the Caribbean . . . all these CLUES are pretty tantalizing!" Colette murmured.

"Mouselets," Paulina said, her snout LIGHTING UP, "maybe someone's telling us where our next adventure will be!"

Just then, the final THEA SISTER entered the room: Nicky!

She HEADED for her friends and pawed them each an envelope.

"This is a plane ticket," said Colette, GLANCING inside.

Nicky nodded. "Uh-huh! And not for just any old **TRIP**. This one's something special. Ready to go to the **BAHAMAS**?!"

She sat back and grinned at her *friends'* amazed expressions. "Okay, so remember when Professor Van Kraken asked for volunteers for a research internship at a **wildlife center**?"

The other mouselets nodded.

"Well, we all assumed it would be here on Whale Island, but . . ."

"Are you saying it's going to be on an **ISLAND** in the Caribbean!?!" Colette cried in disbelief.

"Exactly! The professor called this morning to tell me we've been chosen. He gave me all the *details*. I just booked our travel: We're **flying** to Great Inagua . . .

WHY DIDN'T YOU TELL US?!

Just a few days later, the **THEA SISTERS** were getting ready to depart. The mouselets scurried down from their rooms to head to the airport.

As Pam was trying to squeeze Colette's pink **LUGGAGE** into her SUV, the Thea Sisters' rivals, the Ruby Crew, walked by.

"Hi, Pam," sneered the group's leader, Ruby Flashyfur. "Do you really need all those clothes to work with the slimy **PLANTS** and stinky **animals** here on the island?"

Ruby's friends Alicia, Connie, and Zoe snickered.

"We'll be on an **ISLAND**, all right. Just not this one!" Pam replied with a grin.

"Oh, yeah? And just what nasty spot is the professor sending you off to?" Zoe asked.

"You've got the wrong end of the cheese stick, Zoe," Nicky said, laughing. "We're heading for white beaches, crystal-blue water, palm trees, flamingos . . ."

"Coconuts, pineapples, **exotic fruits** . . ." Pam continued.

"Wh-what in the name of string cheese are you squeaking about?" Connie sputtered.

"The Caribbean!" replied Colette, suddenly appearing with a pink hatbox in her paws. "Sorry, Pam, I forgot this one."

"What?!" Ruby squealed. "You're going to the Caribbean?"

"Uh-huh," said Nicky. "Professor Van Kraken forgot to announce it during class. The biologist who organized this study trip lives in the BAHAMAS. He runs a wildlife

center on Great Inagua, where he cares for the island's **BIRDS**."

"But . . . but . . . that's not possible!" Zoe hissed. "Ruby, why did you tell us not to *apply*?!"

"You said it would be a horrible place full of boring animals!" Connie moaned.

"How was I supposed to know?!" Ruby snapped, tearing at her fur.

"If you'll excuse us, we've got a *FLIGHT* to catch," Nicky said.

The mouselets hopped into the SUV and **took off**, leaving the Ruby Crew behind.

THE BAHAMAS

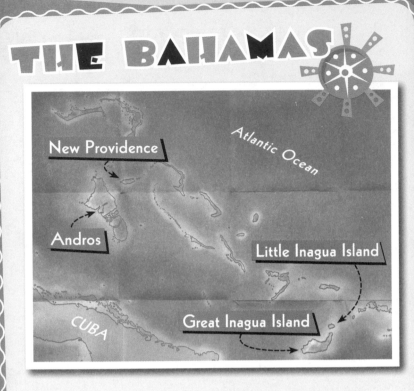

New Providence

Atlantic Ocean

Andros

Little Inagua Island

CUBA

Great Inagua Island

The Bahamas are approximately seven hundred islands located in the Atlantic Ocean near Central America and Cuba. Andros, in the northwest, is the largest island. The capital, Nassau, is located east of Andros on the island of New Providence. The third-largest island in the archipelago is Great Inagua. Next to it is Little Inagua, a small island inhabited only by animals, including many types of birds.

WELCOME!

A few hours later, the Thea Sisters' plane *glided* onto the runway in Matthew Town, on Great Inagua Island.

"That journey felt longer than one of Professor Humdrum's lectures." Nicky sighed, STRETCHING her paws. "I can't wait to take a nice little run on the beach."

"Hold that thought, Nicky," Violet said. "Our first stop is Professor Kendal's **wildlife center**."

"How do we get there?" Pam asked.

"The PROFESSOR is supposed to pick us up. He should be here," Violet replied.

But there was no one waiting for them at the airport. The mouselets **LOOKED** around in vain.

They were a bit grumpy and disgruntled after their long flight. In front of them was a **dusty**, empty road.

Suddenly, the bush behind the Thea Sisters shook, and an animal's nose peeked out from the **leaves**.

"Ahhh!" shouted Colette, almost jumping out of her fur. "**HEEEELP!**"

Paulina giggled behind her paws. "It's just a sweet little donkey, Coco!"

Colette **sniffed**. "A sweet little donkey . . . who's trying to **chew up my new hat!**"

Heeeelp!

Just then, a **BLUE VAN** appeared at the end of the road. It soon **STOPPED** in front of the mouselets. There was a bright pink FLAMINGO painted on the side.

"Hey!" shouted the mouselet behind the wheel, leaning out the window to *wave*. "Welcome, mouselets! Hop in."

The five **friends** had expected a serious professor to pick them up. They exchanged confused looks.

"You're the **STUDENTS** from Mouseford Academy, right?" the ratlet in the passenger seat asked.

"Yes, that's us," Paulina said.

"**PERFECT!** I'm Tamera, and he's Chris," the mouselet explained. "We work together at the wildlife center. We'll take you to Professor Kendal. We're going to have a lot of fun together while you're here."

Tamera waved for them to climb in. There

was a loud 𝓇𝓊𝓂𝒷𝓁𝑒 from the van's old engine, and they were off!

The van was a little battered, and the windows were covered in a layer of **dust**, but that didn't stop the mouselets from admiring the splendid view: blue ocean, white beaches, and a cloudless sky. The Thea Sisters sighed with contentment. It was marvemouse to be surrounded by such gorgeous, unspoiled nature.

"**LOOK** up there!" Paulina squeaked. A large bird with pink FEATHERS was flying over their snouts.

"That's a FLAMINGO," explained Chris. "There are more than eighty thousand of them here on the island. The wildlife center is working to protect them and keep them safe."

"What a magnificent creature," Violet murmured.

"And what a fabumouse **SHADE** of pink!" Colette sighed.

"See that, Coco?" Nicky said with a mischievous grin. "Sometimes nature can be just as brilliant as any fashion designer."

The mouselets laughed.

THEIR ADVENTURE HAD BEGUN!

THE FiRST MiSSioN

A few **minutes** later, the van stopped in front of a low, white building. A green **sign** read:

PINK
FLAMINGO
Wildlife Center

"**WE'RE HERE!**" announced Tamera.

The Thea Sisters piled out of the van. The center's door opened, and a rodent with a large **bag** in his paws ran out, followed by a young mouselet.

"Tamera, thank goodmouse you're back. We need the **VAN** right now!"

"Of course, Professor Kendal," Tamera replied. "Why? What's happened?"

"I just received an emergency call. There's a FLAMINGO with an injured leg that needs our help."

The Thea Sisters exchanged a worried LOOK.

The professor noticed the **mouselets**. "Oh! Pardon me, I had hoped to meet you under better circumstances. I am Professor Kendal, and this is my assistant, Kyla. Unfortunately, we must *hurry off*."

There's an emergency!

"We can come help you," Nicky offered.

"I don't know if that's a **good** idea, Professor," Kyla said. "These mouselets don't know anything about the ISLAND yet. Wouldn't it be better for them to stay here?"

"I'll stay here at the center," said Chris. "And no worries, the mouselets will do just fine."

"Okay," Professor Kendal agreed. "Hop in."

The Thea Sisters joined Tamera, Kyla, and Professor Kendal in the van, which then took them to the shores of a small LAGOON.

As soon as they arrived, an elderly rodent came to meet them. "PROFESSOR, thank goodmouse you're here! The injured FLAMINGO is over there," she said.

"If you ask me, nothing can be done for it," said a ratlet who'd appeared behind her.

"Rik, don't say that!" the elderly rodent replied. "We must take care of our island and *all* its inhabitants."

The ratlet shrugged. "Worrying about this

island is just a waste of time. **Luckily**, I'll be getting out of here soon."

The older rodent shook her snout. "Don't **LISTEN** to my grandson. He always talks like that."

Meanwhile, the professor had silently crept up to the **FLAMINGO**, which was flailing around on the sand, unable to get up.

There's nothing that can be done!

The **THEA SiSTERS** held their breath while he examined the animal's leg. With assistance from Kyla and Tamera, he applied a BANDAGe to the wound.

"This is just a temporary solution," the professor explained when he'd finished. "Now we must take the flamingo to the center, where it can **heal**."

As they were returning to the center, Colette said, "That was **THRILLING**!"

Nicky agreed. "Your wildlife center seems so important for the island."

Tamera smiled, but her expression CLOUDED OVER. "It is . . . but unfortunately it won't be for much longer."

The mouselets **LOOKED** at one

There we go!

another in surprise.

"Tamera is right," the professor explained. "We don't have the funding we need, and we may be forced to **CLOSE**."

"But the flamingos and the other birds . . . what will they do?" asked Paulina, **shocked**.

"There are other wildlife centers on the **iSLaND**," Kyla replied. "Although they don't have the resources to care for all the island's animals . . ."

"What about you? What will you do? Look for work somewhere else?" Violet asked.

Kyla sighed. "We'll try, but I'm afraid it will be very difficult."

"For now, let's not think about it," said Tamera, her **smile** returning.

"WE HAVE A FLAMINGO TO TEND TO!"

MATTERS OF THE HEART

Over the next few days, the Thea Sisters got settled into their work on Great Inagua. Together, the mouselets looked after the **injured** flamingo.

Little by little, the bird made progress, especially thanks to Nicky, who became very attached to it. She called it **BLACK STAR** because there was a small spot on its beak that looked like a star.

When the flamingo had completely healed, the moment came to **RELEASE** it. The Thea Sisters said good-bye, with tears in their eyes.

The mouselets also got to be very friendly

with the researchers at the center, especially Tamera. Colette noticed Tamera was happy whenever she spent time with Chris, and that the RATLET glanced at her often.

Colette loved playing matchmouser. "Something tells me there's more than just FRiENDSHiP between Tamera and Chris," she told the other Thea Sisters.

"Are you sure?" asked Nicky, who hadn't noticed anything.

"Believe me, mouselets: I am an expert when it

Bye, Black Star!

comes to recognizing the **SIGNS** of a crush!"

"We know, Coco," said Violet, winking. "You are a true detective when it comes to matters of the **heart**."

That night, just before they **LEFT** the wildlife center, the Thea Sisters witnessed something that confirmed Colette's suspicions. Tamera **went** into the laboratory, where Chris was analyzing a specimen of seawater. "Chris, do you have a minute? I **brought you something . . .**"

The ratlet smiled at her. "Yes, I've just finished. And I have **something** for you, too . . ."

A moment later, they'd pulled out identical **books** — *Stories and Legends of Inagua* — and shyly pawed them to each other. When they realized their gifts were the same, their whiskers wavered with **embarrassment** and they both giggled.

"Good call, Coco," Violet said, smiling. "Your instinct was **right on**!"

Soon Chris left. When Tamera joined the Thea Sisters, she looked **sad**.

"Hey, what's wrong?" Paulina asked.

Tamera shook her snout. "Nothing . . ."

"Um, when a mouselet says 'nothing' in that tone, I'm pretty sure it actually means 'something'," said Colette, reaching out a paw to her new *friend*.

Pam smiled at Tamera. "If you need help, you can count on us! I swear it on a stack of cheese slices."

Tamera gave her a shy smile. "Well, to tell you the truth, it's about Chris . . ."

"I **thought** so," replied Colette. "I know you like him . . . and he likes you, too!"

Tamera sighed. "That's where you're wrong. I really like Chris, but he doesn't seem to think about me at all."

"How can that be?" Colette **spluttered**. "He's always glancing over at you!"

"*Maybe*," the mouselet murmured. "But he only thinks of me as a colleague. Every time I ask him to do something outside work, he **AVOIDS** me. Tonight I asked him if he wanted to grab a bite to eat, but he told me that he'd rather go home and **record** his research."

The **mouselets** shared a look of surprise.

"And he keeps saying he'll **HAVE** to leave the island because of the center's funding problems," continued Tamera. "Today he told me he's going on a **job** interview in a few days. If he transfers, we won't **see** each other anymore." Tamera buried her snout in her paws to hide her t e a r s.

He doesn't care about me!

The **THEA SISTERS** gathered around Tamera and **comforted** her. Colette grew **PENSIVE**. Could it be that her instinct for affairs of the heart was off?

PIRATE ATTACK!

The next day was Saturday, which meant the Thea Sisters' first WeeKeND in the BAHAMAS had come at last.

The wildlife center was closed. Professor Kendal suggested the mouselets take a trip to one of the other islands.

But Colette, Nicky, Pam, Paulina, and Violet had decided to spend their **FREE** days with Tamera. Their new friend had told them about a **HISTORICAL REENACTMENT** of pirates landing on Great Inagua. Tamera had the **LEAD** role in the production.

So the mouselets **AGREED** to go with Tamera to see Angelica, the **elderly rodent** they'd met on their first day. She was like a grandmother to Tamera, and she'd offered to help with her costume.

"Tell us more about this reenactment. I've always loved a good pirate story!" said Nicky as they scampered toward Angelica's house, just outside Matthew Town.

Tamera smiled and told her tale. "It all began on a DARK AND STORMY night. A galleon* as black as thunderclouds dropped anchor in the bay. It belonged to the PIRATE ANNABEL, famouse over all the seas for her ferocity. When she and her crew invaded the island, there was no one brave enough to stand up to them."

The mouselets shivered.

"What a thrilling tale!" Paulina whispered.

"Annabel had her eye on one thing: the TREASURE that belonged to the island's governor," Tamera continued. "So she went straight to the palace and stole all the JEWELS

---

* A galleon is a large, stately sailing ship used in the fifteenth to eighteenth centuries.

and **gold** she could find. And she mousenapped James, the governor's son. She brought him on board her ship, which sailed **swiftly** away from the island. And then . . ."

Meanwhile, the mouselets had arrived in front of a small wooden house.

"Then . . . ?!" asked Colette, who was following the story **breathlessly**. "What happened next?"

Tamera laughed. "At that point, history becomes **legend**. No one knows the truth. All we know is that a few days later, **Annabel** returned to Great Inagua for unknown reasons. Before

What a thrilling tale!

She stole everything!

she could drop anchor, a terrible storm hit. The crew was shipwrecked, and the governor's son managed to escape. He REACHED the island, but all traces of Annabel were lost. So was the stolen treasure."

Another squeak startled the mouselets. "Actually, Annabel's reason for RETURNING to

THE PIRATE ANNABEL

Inagua wasn't *that* mysterious."

Granny Angelica appeared from behind the house. She was carrying a basket full of COCONUTS.

JAMES, THE GOVERNOR'S SON

"Granny Angelica!" **CRIED** Tamera. "We came for —"

"Annabel's **costume**. I know, my dear," replied the rodent with a

Come on in!

Hi, Angelica!

smile. She opened the door to her house. "Come on in."

Inside the house, it was cool and DIM. Angelica offered them pieces of fresh COCONUT.

Biting into one, Pam asked, "Excuse me, but" — chomp — "what were you going to say before about Annabel? Do you" — chomp — "know her reason for returning to Inagua?"

Angelica SMiLED. "Oh, of course! Annabel returned for the oldest reason there is: love!"

A FREE HEART

The mouselets gave Granny Angelica a CURIOUS look.

"What's love got to do with it?" Pam asked.

"LOVE has everything to do with it, my dear mouselet," replied the rodent. "Annabel had been an orphan since she was just a wee mouseling, and she was raised by a **PIRATE**. That's how she became a pirate herself. But she had a *noble* spirit. In all her years as a buccaneer, she never stole from the poor — only the rich. And she never hurt anyone."

"But we know she mousenapped James, the governor's **SON**," Colette objected.

"That's true," said Angelica. "She intended to **FREE** him a few days later, but after spending a few hours together, something blossomed in Annabel's heart. She fell hopelessly in LOVE with James!"

"*How romantic!*" whispered Colette.

"Annabel decided to take him back HOME," continued Granny Angelica. "The ratlet seemed to return her love, but Annabel wanted him to be free to choose. He could follow his **heart** and remain with her, or return to his former life.

"Now, we can only imagine how James would have chosen.

As Tamera told you, a **TERRIBLE** storm divided these two star-crossed lovers . . ."

The mouselets' eyes shone with **FEELING**. Tamera in particular was moved by this romantic story. But she seemed **SAD**, too. "How do you know that's what happened?" she asked Angelica.

"In those days, one of my ancestors worked at the palace," explained Granny Angelica. "Sir James himself told him everything!"

"**Sizzling spark plugs!**" cried Pam. "What an incredible story."

Granny Angelica pointed to a large **TRUNK**. "Open it, Tamera. Inside you'll find what you're looking for."

When the mouselet raised the heavy **WOODEN** lid, her jaw dropped. Inside was a **splendid** red velvet coat.

"But this . . ." she began, taking it out.

"Yes, it's Annabel's **coat**," Angelica said. "James was **CLUTCHING** it to his chest when he was rescued after the shipwreck. I believe he tried to keep Annabel close during the storm to **PROTECT** her . . . but he was left with only her coat. James gave it to my ancestor.

But this . . .

He knew his family would never accept the **truth** — that he had fallen in love with a pirate. So my ancestor kept his secret safe. Since then my **family** has passed down her coat and her story from generation to generation."

Angelica smiled at Tamera. "This is the first time I've ever told the sad **STORY** of

Annabel. And this is the right moment to use her coat!" She tousled Tamera's fur affectionately. "**Wear it** on the day of the reenactment. I'm so happy that you're **PLAYING** Annabel. You have her courage and her strength."

The mouselet held the coat tightly to her chest. "Thank you, Granny Angelica.

IT WILL BE AN HONOR!"

SNIP AND SEW

The mouselets said good-bye to Granny Angelica and HEADED back to town.

"What an amazing story," Paulina said thoughtfully.

"Yes," replied Violet. "They found love, only to lose it again . . ."

"They lost a lot of things in that story," Pam said.

Colette LOOKED confused. "What do you mean, Pam?"

"The governor's TREASURE was lost, too, right?"

Nicky nodded. "You're right! I wonder what happened to it."

"It's a mystery," replied Tamera. "It probably went down with the ship during the

storm. **DIVERS** have searched the bottom of the sea around the island, but no one has ever found a trace of it."

"And so it remains part of the **legend**," concluded Violet.

"In any case, mouselets," exclaimed Colette, her tone suddenly light, "we have a mission to complete!"

"What **mission**, Coco?" Nicky asked. "Finding the treasure?"

Her friend burst out laughing. "No, not that. We've got to complete Tamera's pirate costume!"

At her friends' **SURPRISED** expressions, Colette sighed. "Don't you see? Granny Angelica gave us Annabel's **coat**, but Tamera also needs pants, a shirt, a hat, boots —"

"Slow down, sister, **we get it!**" Pam interrupted her. "But where are we going to find all that?"

Colette **smiled**. "I saw a bunch of little shops in town that should do the trick . . . let's shake a tail!"

And so, for the rest of the day, Colette dragged her friends into shops all over

Pants, shirt, hat, boots . . .

Matthew Town. They gathered old clothes, fabric, and tons of **accessories**.

In the late afternoon, they made their final stop at Tamera's house.

"Thank goodmouse we're done!" cried Pam, falling into a chair. "Today my paws have traveled more MILES than my SUV."

Tamera had already begun trying on her purchases. She was marveling at Colette's STYLE skills. "You have a special eye for clothes, Colette." She twirled around. "Dressed like this, I really look like the pirate Annabel!"

Colette shook her snout thoughtfully. "Hmm, that coat is a little BIG on you. But don't worry, I can make it smaller."

She carefully began ripping out one of the COAT'S seams. A scroll of **paper** fell out of the lining.

"What's this?" asked Pam, unrolling the yellowed paper.

It was covered with DRAWINGS, now faded, in the shapes of islands and various other symbols.

"Hey . . . those are the islands in the BAHAMAS!" cried Tamera.

On the back of the map was written:

Dear James,

Go to my hideout, climb up onto the flat rock, and look east. Before the sun sets, you'll find the treasure. Take it — it belongs to you, as my heart belongs to you.

Your Annabel

"SISTERS, are you thinking what I'm thinking?" asked Pam.

Colette nodded. "This is Annabel's treasure map!"

¡ BELİEVE!

Tamera took the yellowed paper in her paws. "I can't believe it! This map could lead us to the treasure! We've got to show it to Chris."

Quick as the mouse who ran up the clock, the six mouselets headed for the ratlet's house.

Along the **ROAD**, Tamera turned over the parchment in her paws. She was so distracted, she ran right into a rodent walking toward them with her paws full of packages.

"**OOPS!**" Tamera cried. Both mice tumbled to the ground.

"Kyla!" said Colette, recognizing the mouselet who worked with Professor Kendal.

"Sorry about that," cried Tamera, helping

her colleague gather up the **FRUIT** that had fallen from her packages.

"Got your snout in the clouds?" Kyla **MUTTERED**.

Tamera nodded. She began telling her friend the story of their incredible discovery. She even showed Kyla the **map**.

Kyla examined it for a long time. "What a stroke of luck," she said. "Now excuse me, I must go make **DINNER**."

The Thea Sisters and Tamera said good-bye and continued toward Chris's house. They found him on the porch, playing his ukulele* and singing.

"I didn't know Chris was a **musician**," Pam said.

Tamera smiled. "He's singing an old song

* A ukulele is a musical instrument like a guitar but smaller and with only four strings.

about the legend of our **pirate**."

"Mouselets, what are you doing here?" Chris greeted them. "I thought you were going to **visit** the other islands."

"They stayed on Great Inagua to help me with my costume," explained Tamera. "And squeaking of which, look what we found!" She **eagerly** pawed him the map.

Chris examined it. "What is it? It looks like a **treasure map** . . ."

Tamera nodded. "Yes, it's for the governor's treasure stolen by the pirate **Annabel**!"

For a moment, Chris's whiskers stood on end. Then he burst out **laughing**. "This is a joke, right?"

Colette spoke up. "It's not a joke! It really is a **treasure map**, drawn by Annabel herself!"

"Oh, really? So where did you find it?" asked Chris.

"In Annabel's coat," Nicky said. "Angelica gave it to us."

Chris shook his snout. "Granny Angelica is wonderful, but she has quite an imagination. Do you really think she has Annabel's actual coat? And her actual treasure map?"

"She does!" Tamera insisted. "Sir James himself gave the coat to her ancestor. And the map was inside!"

"Tamera," said Chris seriously, "you don't really believe the pirate sewed a treasure map inside her coat and that it's stayed hidden until now?"

"Why not? Is it so unbelievable?"

Violet cleared her throat. "Um, actually . . . it's unlikely the map could survive the fury of the storm —"

"Come on, Vi, have a little FAITH! It might be unlikely, but it's not impossible, right?" Colette interrupted.

"Maybe we should ask an **expert** to examine it," Paulina suggested. "Someone who could tell us how old it is."

"That's a good idea," said Nicky. "What do you say, Tamera?"

For a moment, Tamera was quiet as a mouse. "I'll tell you what I believe," she SAID at last. "I believe that Annabel hid the governor's treasure, that she drew the map and CONCEALED it in her coat, and that now the map is in my paws."

Tamera pointed to the writing on the back. "Read here! Annabel wanted to leave this map for James. But unfortunately, things didn't go as she'd planned. She . . . I . . . I must do everything I can to find the treasure! It could change our DeSTINY . . ." she trailed off.

Chris shook his snout. "You're such a dreamer, Tamera. This map won't change our destiny."

"Believe what you want, but I'm going to find that TREASURE!" Tamera insisted.

"Tamera, you're getting your tail in a twist over nothing!" Chris cried. "You'll drag us who-knows-where to search for treasure that probably doesn't even exist —"

"I'm not asking you to come with me. I'll go by myself!" Tamera said. Her snout had turned redder than a cheese rind, and there were tears in her eyes. Before the THEA SïSTERS could react, she'd turned and RUN away.

"Tamera! Wait!" shouted Colette, starting to follow her friend.

Chris stopped her. "Let her go. Believe me, **I KNOW** Tamera well. Sometimes she gets carried away. But eventually she gets her **paws on the ground** again. Tomorrow we'll be able to reason with her."

With a **sigh**, Colette remained on the porch. Soon, Tamera was as small as a cheese crumb in the **distance**.

A STUBBORN MOUSELET

That evening at **dinner**, the Thea Sisters couldn't stop thinking about the map. Even Pam, who never let anything distract her from a good meal, had trouble focusing on her food.

"The governor's TREASURE would be very valuable today, right?" she asked.

"Yes. If we find it, we could use the money to keep Professor Kendal's wildlife center from 𝕔𝕝𝕠𝕤𝕚𝕟𝕘," Nicky said.

"Maybe that's what Tamera was thinking when she mentioned destiny," said Violet. "Coco, did you manage to track her down?"

Colette shook her snout. "She isn't answering her PHONE."

"Tomorrow we'll go by her place and get to the bottom of this *story*," Nicky declared.

"Great idea. But not till around noon, okay? I need to **sleep in**!" said Violet, yawning. The others burst out laughing. Violet was a notorious sleepysnout!

But Violet's plans for a late start were rudely interrupted. Shortly after dawn the

Tomorrow we'll get to the bottom of this!

next morning, there was a loud **BANGING** outside the mouselets' door.

BOOM, BOOM, BOOM!

Nicky was the first one to wake up. It sounded like there was a marching band outside! Then she realized someone was knocking on the door.

"Yawn . . . what's going on?" groaned Colette, running a paw through her fur.

Nicky went to open the door. "Chris! Is everything okay?" she asked in surprise.

Chris burst into the room like a mouse being chased by a pack of hungry cats. Then, realizing the mouselets were still in their pajamas, he blushed from the tip of his snout to the tip of his tail. "I'm sorry, **mouselets**, I . . . I didn't realize it was so early . . ."

"Did you bring us **breakfast**?" Pam asked.

"I probably should have, but unfortunately I'm here for another reason . . . Tamera is MISSING!"

Now the **MOUSELETS** were wide awake.

"How can that be?" Colette cried.

"I found this *note* under my door," Chris explained, showing it to them.

Dear Chris,

I know that you disapprove, and that makes me unhappy, but I MUST go find the treasure. I've decided to follow the map, and nothing you say will stop me. I know you'll worry about me, but don't be afraid: I'll manage! I promise to keep my phone on so you can reach me.

See you soon,
Tamera

P.S. I'm going to Annabel's hideout . . . I think the treasure is there!

"Do you know when she dropped this off?" Violet asked.

"Last night, I think . . . she must have left this morning at first **light**. And now she's not answering her phone. Who knows where she's gone!" Chris wailed. He put his snout in his paws. "That **MOUSELET** is so stubborn! I can't believe she went off in search of a legendary pirate **treasure**!"

"Don't worry, we'll help you find her," Colette said.

"I know she took her boat; I checked. I'm **worried** she went alone. Something might happen to her!"

"It's going to be okay, Chris. We'll **HELP** you," Violet assured him. "First we'll figure out where she went, and then . . ."

GRROOOWWL

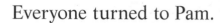

Everyone turned to Pam.

"Crumbling cheesecake, don't look at me like that. I can't help it; it's just my **STOMACH**!" Pam said. "I want to find Tamera, too, but how about some breakfast first?"

Even Chris had to crack a smile. He and the mouselets scurried off to prepare for their *MISSION*.

CLUES!

TAMERA WENT TO ANNABEL'S HIDEOUT. WHERE COULD THAT BE? IS IT A PLACE MARKED ON THE MAP?

WiTH A LiTTLE LUCK . . .

After a big breakfast of **fruit**, Chris and the Thea Sisters hopped into the **wildlife center's** van and hurried down to Great Inagua's port. From there, they would follow Tamera's trail in Chris's sailboat.

There was just one LITTLE PROBLEM: No one knew which way she had gone!

"Chris, are you sure leaving in such a hurry is a **G°°D iDEA**?" asked Violet.

"What are we supposed to do?! Stay here and wait while Tamera runs into who knows what kind of **DANGER**?!" cried Chris, turning red to the roots of his fur.

Violet was squeakless, and the ratlet *apologized* immediately. "Sorry, Violet, I didn't mean to snap at you. I'm just worried about Tamera."

"We understand, Chris. But let's take a moment and think this out," suggested Nicky.

Chris nodded and began to squeak more calmly. "Okay, so if Tamera **LEFT** at dawn, she would only be about an hour ahead of us. We could try to catch sight of her if we head **NORTH** . . . and then turn to the **east** . . . or . . ."

The mouselets exchanged a *worried* look.

"And then, if we're lucky . . ." Chris's squeak trailed off hopelessly.

"If we're very lucky," said Violet, "someone at the port saw her **SHOVE OFF** and might know which **DIRECTION** she headed in."

We'll ask at the port!

"Good thought, Vi," cried Nicky. "Someone must have seen her!"

Unfortunately, **no one** at the port could help them. One sailor confirmed he'd seen a mouselet depart that morning, but he didn't notice which direction she'd sailed in.

"But it's STRANGE," added the sailor. "You aren't the first to ask me if I saw a mouselet leaving this morning."

Chris and the Thea Sisters exchanged a look of ALARM.

"What do you mean?" asked Chris.

"After your friend left, I talked to a ratlet who seemed like he was in a big RUSH to join her," the sailor explained.

"And then?" asked Colette, urging him on.

"And then **NOTHING**," the sailor said, shrugging. "I told him I didn't know which way she'd gone."

"Can you describe this ratlet?" asked Chris.

"Hmm, let's see . . . He was tall, but not too tall, not **HEAVY**, but not THIN . . . Oh, he was wearing a **YELLOW** shirt. I don't remember anything else, I'm afraid."

After they'd thanked the sailor, Chris and the mouselets took a moment to plan their next move.

"Well, that description wasn't too helpful," said Paulina.

"You can say that again, sister!" Pam agreed. "Not heavy, not tall . . . It could be anyone."

"But why would someone want to follow Tamera?" asked Nicky.

"Keep calm and scurry on, rodents!"

cried Colette. "We can **worry** about it later. The most important thing now is to find her. Let's think for a minute. Tamera's *note* said that she would go to Annabel's hideout . . . but where could that be?"

Violet **lit up**. "Paulina, you took a picture of the map with your cell phone, right? Let's take a look."

Her friend pulled out her phone, and they all gathered around to examine the **PHOTO**.

"There it is!" Colette suddenly cried. "Tamera must have gone there."

She pointed to a small island near Great Inagua. It was marked with a picture of a **GALLEON** with a big *A* on the side.

"You're right, Coco," said Nicky. "The *A* must stand for Annabel — this is her ship, and this island must be the location of her secret hideout."

"Okay," said Chris, studying the map. "The island is **north** of Great Inagua. Come on, there's no time to lose . . . Let's make like a cheese wheel and roll!"

ALL ABOARD!

As soon as he set paw on the sailboat, Chris was transformed. In place of the gawky, young ratlet was an experienced, **CONFIDENT** sailor.

He assigned each mouselet a task. "We need someone agile and brave to **climb** the mast."

"I'll do it!" said Nicky, who already knew the basics of sailing.

"Good. Then someone else can manage the sails and the LINES . . ."

"Those are the ropes," Nicky explained to her friends, who looked a little **confused**.

"Violet and I can do that," said Colette.

"And someone should stay with me at the **helm** and help me with the navigation system."

Paulina immediately volunteered. "I'll take care of the **TECHNICAL** part."

"And me?" asked Pam.

"You can be the first mate, Pam. On a boat like this, there's always something to do."

"Okay," Pam agreed. She grinned. "I'll start by making SANDWICHES for our first snack!"

As the morning sun began to **warm up** the air, Chris steered the ship out of the small port. When they were on the open OCEAN, he showed the mouselets how to arrange the sails.

"In these waters, you need to pay attention to the depth of the sea," he explained. Then his snout **DARKENED** for a moment. "I hope Tamera was careful . . ."

The mouselets were silent as they sailed, each FOCUSED on the task their friend had assigned them. The boat skipped across the surface of the turquoise sea as the wind blew gently against the white sails.

Suddenly, Nicky pointed to a spot on the horizon. "There's something over there . . . I think it's a big ROCK."

Paulina checked the ship's instruments and SHOOK her snout. "No, it should be all clear there . . ."

"It's a ship!" Colette cried.

Chris left the rudder in Paulina's paws and RAN to the prow. "It's Tamera!" he shouted.

Little by little, they drew CLOSE enough to get a glimpse of their FRIEND, who waved them over. A few minutes later, they were right next to her boat.

"Hi, guys!" Tamera shouted. "What are you doing out here in the middle of the ocean?"

"We were looking for you! What are *you* doing out here in the middle of the ocean?" asked Nicky.

"I — well, I'm having a little trouble . . ." explained Tamera, clearing her throat.

"I knew it!" Chris burst out. "It was reckless to go out on your own!"

"It's not my fault," Tamera protested. "My GPS is broken, and I couldn't find the right course for the island."

Chris jumped onto Tamera's boat and examined its instruments. "That's weird. We used your boat two days ago, and everything was working perfectly. Now the GPS and the radio are both broken!"

"So you see, it wasn't my fault," Tamera

replied, crossing her paws. A moment later, she **softened**. "Anyway, thanks for coming to find me."

"We were worried," Chris said. "But the important thing is you're okay."

The two rodents smiled, looking into each other's EYES.

Anyway . . . thanks!

"Ahem." Colette cleared her throat. "Sorry, but shouldn't we decide what to do next?"

Chris shook his snout. "Of course. Let's all get on board my boat and go home."

Tamera put her paws on her hips. "What do you mean? I have no intention of turning back. Not until we've found Annabel's treasure!"

"Tamera, I know you don't want to give up on your plan," Chris said. "But I have my interview in Haiti tomorrow. I can't come with you, and you really shouldn't go on this adventure alone."

We'll be with her!

"She's not alone," said Nicky. "We'll be with her!"

"That's right," the others agreed.

"Really?" Tamera asked hopefully.

The Thea Sisters exchanged **LOOKS**. "Of course!"

Chris sighed. "Okay, then. But you don't have the **EQUIPMENT** . . ."

"I have my GPS," Paulina said. "That should do."

Chris couldn't think of any more objections. Reluctantly, he climbed back onto his boat.

"Sail safely!" he said.

The mouselets nodded and scampered over to Tamera's **BOAT**. Soon they were

READY TO SET SAIL AGAIN.

STRAIGHT TO THE PIRATE'S HIDEOUT!

The journey to the island went off without a hitch. The sailboat glided lightly across the waves, throwing little sprays of sea foam in its wake.

Now and then, Tamera gave orders to her crew. "Take in the sails!" the mouselet shouted, and Nicky quickly pulled on a line at the corner of one sail, which was billowing in the wind.

"Prepare to tack," Tamera declared. "Come on, mouselets, if we continue at this SPEED, we'll see the island in no time."

"Aye, aye, Cap'n," said Paulina.

"Tamera's like a pirate at the helm of her galleon," Colette said.

The mouselets giggled. They felt like they were traveling through time!

A few minutes later, Tamera consulted the old map and then checked Paulina's **GPS**. "Let's turn west. Annabel's hideout can't be far."

She was right. Soon they were approaching a little island with **HIGH**, **ROCKY** cliffs reaching up toward the sky. Here and there were sandy beaches surrounded by steep, **THICK** rocks.

For a moment, the mouselets stopped to admire this enchanting place. The sea seemed clearer here, and the sand was a lovely shade of pink.

"It's so *beautiful*!" Colette murmured.

"Yes, but there's just sand and stones here," noted Pam, gazing at the **ROCKS** that

covered the ISLAND'S surface. "Where could Annabel's HIDEOUT be?"

Tamera SMILED. "Pam, I think you're forgetting something. A pirate doesn't need a hideout for herself, but for her ship."

"You're right!" cried Violet. "So we need to look for a cave."

"A cave that's hidden," added Colette, "where Annabel could stay without being seen . . ."

Tamera guided the ship around the island, but they didn't see anything that looked like an entrance to a CAVE.

"How can this be?" she said. "There must be an opening somewhere in the rock . . ."

The THEA SISTERS sighed with disappointment. It looked like Chris was right — the map was just someone's mean joke!

"Look!" Nicky **squeaked** suddenly, following the *flight* of two seagulls across the sky. "Those gulls came from a POINT behind those rocks . . . over there!"

"Let's go see," said Tamera, turning the ship.

When they were just a few yards from the CLIFFS, the mouselets found a large stone in the water right in front of an opening in the rocks.

"Way to go, Nicky!" cried Paulina. "We would never have found the cave if you hadn't spotted those birds."

"Let's go, sisters!" Pam said.

"THE TREASURE IS WAITING!"

A SPOOKY HIDEOUT

Tamera stopped Pam. "**WAIT!** We better leave the sailboat here and use the raft. Otherwise, the sailboat will get damaged on those rocks. The raft can **move** more deftly and safely."

She dropped anchor and **STOPPED** the boat. A moment later, the six mouselets were on board the **raft**. They passed swiftly through the cave's entrance. The massive cliffs seemed to press in on them as they slipped down a damp, dark passage.

"Brr!" said Colette. "This place gives me the shivers."

As they glided along, the scene before them transformed, leaving the friends breathless. An immense grotto opened up in front of them. The sunlight filtered down from an opening above, tossing golden REFLECTIONS onto the water.

"Holey cheese," Colette marveled. "Annabel chose a really magical place for her hideout."

While Tamera tied the raft to a rock, the Thea Sisters looked around, enchanted by the cave's natural beauty.

Nicky was the first to clamber out and climb up onto a rock. She pointed to a wide, rocky surface in the distance. "Look! That must be the flat rock that Annabel wrote about."

"You're right," said Colette. "It's the only **flat** rock."

Tamera's tail was trembling. "So far, everything we've discovered has matched what Annabel wrote on her map, so that must mean . . ."

"There could really be treasure here!" Colette finished. "Come on, mouselets, let's find out!"

Nicky helped the others **SCRAMBLE OUT** of the raft. Then she headed for the flat rock.

"I don't see anything here . . ." she said, looking around the stone's **smooth** surface.

When the others reached her, they felt like rats **lost** in a maze. They didn't know what they were looking for.

"Let's read what Annabel wrote again," suggested Violet.

Tamera read from the map. "'Before the sun sets, you'll find the treasure.'"

"There's still a little time before **SUNSET**, but —" Violet began.

OOOOOOOHHHHHH!

A bone-chilling cry echoed through the cave, making the mouselets **JUMP** like a bunch of gerbil babies.

"Wh-what was th-that?" asked Pam. "It sounded like a ghost!"

Paulina giggled. "There's no such thing as **GHOSTS**, Pam! Maybe it's an animal . . ."

What was that?

But another cry interrupted her, sending shivers down her tail.

The **mouselets** drew closer together, sharing a look of fear.

Could the cave be haunted?

TWO SURPRISES

The Thea Sisters and Tamera clutched at one another's paws as the eerie **CRIES** continued.

"It's so creepy . . ." murmured Violet.

Tamera looked *around* carefully. Then a slow smile spread across her snout. "I just figured it out, mouselets. It's not a **GHOST** — it's the wind! When it blows across those rocks over there, it makes that **SPOOKY** sound," she said.

The Thea Sisters still looked more nervous than mice in a lion's den. So

There we go!

Tamera placed her SWEATSHIRT over the opening to keep the air from passing through. The cries immediately stopped. "See, what did I tell you?"

"Better," said Pam, who was a bit rattled. "That sound gave me GOOSE BUMPS!"

Colette put a paw around her **friend's** shoulders. "Snout up, Pam!" She turned to the others. "Let's EXAMINE this rock carefully. If Annabel led us here, it means there's something to find."

"You're right, Coco," Nicky replied. She started inspecting the area.

But no matter how carefully they searched, the mouselets couldn't find anything. After a few minutes, they got DISCOURAGED.

"This is harder than finding a cheese crumb in a haystack," said Pam.

"It's tough to find something when you

don't know what you're looking for," Violet said with a sigh of frustration.

Colette nodded. "Maybe we made a **mistake**. Maybe this isn't the right rock . . . **HEY!**" she stopped. "Did you hear that noise?"

Did you hear that?

The mouselets shook their snouts.

"Is it the *wind* again?" Nicky asked.

"No, it's something else. It sounds like **pawsteps** . . ."

"Your **imagination** must be playing tricks on you, Coco," said Violet. "We're the only ones here."

"Hey, look! The **sun** is just starting to set," Paulina squealed. A ray of sunlight had suddenly fallen on a spot in front of them.

"Check this out, mouselings!" said Paulina.

Her friends joined her in the **CENTER** of the flat rock. When they looked in the right **DIRECTION**, they let out squeaks of surprise. "Ohhhh!"

The sunlight REFLECTED on a rock jutting out of the water, making it look like a big flamingo.

"Crusty cheese chunks!" cried Pam. "It's like magic."

"'Climb up onto the flat rock, and look east,'" said Colette, quoting the note on the back of the map. "This is what Annabel was talking about!"

"Yeah," Paulina agreed. "But what does it mean? The TREASURE can't be there . . ."

"Maybe it's a **clue** that points to the next step, like a treasure hunt," Colette guessed.

Violet opened Annabel's map and studied

it. A smile **lit up** her snout. "I've got it! It must mean we should go to the island with the **FLAMINGO** symbol — Little Inagua!"

"You must be right!" cried Paulina.

Tamera's eyes widened. "I can't believe it . . . We were so close to the treasure and we didn't realize it! Little Inagua is right next to Great Inagua."

"Come on, then; let's **HEAD BACK** to the sailboat and check it out," Violet proposed.

Oh no! What now?

But when the mouselets returned to the **raft**, an unfortunate surprise was waiting for them. There was a huge gash in one side, and the raft was bobbing *limply* in the water!

WE'RE TRAPPED!

The mouselets STARED in dismay at the raft. It was completely unusable!

"But . . . but . . . how could this happen?" asked Paulina.

"Maybe when we steered into the cave, we bumped against a sharp rock without realizing it," Colette suggested.

Tamera shook her snout. "No, I was very careful. Besides, if we'd hit a rock, we would have felt it."

"I'm afraid there's another explanation," Nicky said gravely. She was examining the raft. "A hole this size couldn't be caused by a rock."

"What do you mean?" asked Paulina, alarmed.

"The fabric has been slashed, probably with a knife," Nicky said. "Take a look. The cut is so narrow, plus it's on the part of the raft that stays above *water*. So it couldn't have been made by an underwater rock."

Paulina looked shocked. "But then that means that . . ."

"We're not alone!" concluded Tamera, lowering her squeak. She **LOOKED** around nervously. "Colette, you were right when you said you heard pawsteps . . ."

A tense silence fell over the mouselets.

It was slashed!

Just a few moments ago, this place had seemed full of magic and **wonder**. Now it felt ominous, full of danger and mystery.

Paulina was the first to *squeak*. "How are we going to get out of here without a raft?"

"Maybe we could **SWIM** to the sailboat," suggested Nicky, who was the most athletic in the group.

Tamera shook her snout hopelessly. "That's impossible. It's very far, and the current is strong!"

"So does that mean we're **TRAPPED** here?" Pam asked nervously.

The mouselets were afraid to answer. The only reply came from the wind, which started blowing hard, filling the cave with spooky cries.

"Keep calm! Keep calm!" Colette chanted, reaching for her friends' **paws**. "Let's try to think of a way out."

"There's nothing to think about," Violet said despairingly. "We need a miracle!"

"Like a rescue?" asked Pam, pointing to the entrance of the CAVE. "Look!"

The mouselets followed Pam's paw. The SHAPE of a raft was backlit by the setting sun. They couldn't tell who was on board.

"It could be the sneak who sabotaged our raft," Tamera warned them. "Let's **hide** behind that rock."

But before the mouselets could take a step, they heard a shout from the **raft**. "Tamera! Mouselets! Are you here?"

"It's Chris!" cried Tamera. She waved her paws to get his attention. "Chris, we're over here!"

A few minutes later, the ratlet had joined his friends on the rock. Tamera leaped into his paws. "Oh, Chris! You don't know how happy I am to see you!"

Oh, Chris!

The ratlet hugged her back, but Tamera stepped away, suddenly **embarrassed** by this tender moment.

"I don't understand," she said. "Why are you here? Didn't you have to go back for the interview in **Haiti**?"

Her friend nodded. "Yes, but as I was sailing, I started remembering the **stories** my grandpa told me when I was little."

Tamera and the mouselets looked puzzled.

"My grandpa said the **waters** north of Great Inagua were filled with danger and mystery," Chris continued. "According to ancient legend, there's an island inhabited only by ghosts who make strange, mournful cries."

"Your grandpa was right — this is the mysterious **iSLaND**," said Tamera. "Listen to that **racket**!" Then her squeak grew serious. "So you came back because you were **worried**?"

The ratlet turned pinker than a cat's nose. "I knew that those stories were just **made up**, but . . . yes, I was worried about you . . . um, that is, **all of you** . . ."

"What about your interview?" asked the mouselet.

Chris took her paws in his. "While I was on my way here, I *realized* I'm not really interested in that interview. I'm interested in **you**, Tamera."

I want you to follow your dreams . . .

She blushed, but there was no time to **reply** before Chris went on. "You don't have to say anything. I feel like a total **cheesebrain** for leaving you. I didn't come back just because I was **worried**. I realized I want you to follow your dreams . . . and I want to follow them with you."

The two young mice *smiled* and took each other's paws.

"From now on, I'm sticking to you closer than a glue trap," Chris said.

Tamera laughed. They would have kept on gazing at each other if Nicky hadn't **coughed** loudly. "Um . . . sorry to interrupt, but if we want to sail while there's still **light**, we'd better get going."

"Of course, of course!" **CRIED** Tamera. "Little Inagua awaits! Chris, I'll explain everything on the way. For now, we need to get back to your boat. We'll come back for mine tomorrow."

A POSSIBLE ENEMY

Once they'd **CLIMBED** aboard Chris's boat, the mouselets explained everything that had happened since they'd gone their separate ways: how they'd discovered the hidden **cave**, spotted the rock shaped like a flamingo, and then realized their raft had been **sabotaged**.

Once Chris heard the mouselets' tale, he was convinced the map Tamera had found was authentic. "So the TREASURE must be real!" he breathed.

That made him even more worried about the **DANGER** the mouselets had run into. "If I hadn't decided to come back, you'd still be stuck in that cave. Someone is following you, and they'll do anything to get to the treasure before you!"

"But how is that POSSIBLE? We didn't see anyone following us," Tamera replied.

"Maybe Chris is right," said Nicky slowly. "Whoever sabotaged your raft might be the same mouse who tampered with the **radio** and the **GPS** on your boat."

Tamera **shivered**. Until that moment,

Someone is following you!

But how?

she'd believed her radio and GPS had just malfunctioned. She hadn't connected it to the sabotage of the raft.

"So someone is **tracking** us," she said. "And obviously they want to keep us from reaching our destination . . ."

"Exactly," Chris said, nodding.

"MOLDY MOZZARELLA!" cried Pam. "Who could it be?"

Chris and the mouselets just looked at one another. No one had any ideas.

"Someone must have discovered we were *hunting* for treasure," said Violet. She turned to Tamera. "When you left the port, did you tell anyone where you were going?"

Tamera looked more confused than a cat in a dog kennel. "No, I didn't squeak to anyone."

Colette noticed Chris was chewing his

whiskers with **worry**.

"What's **wrong**, Chris?" she asked.

He shrugged. "I just thought of something, but I'm not sure it makes any sense . . ."

"Go on — it could be **IMPORTANT!**" Colette urged him.

Chris sighed. "While I was heading for the island, I **Spotted** Rik on his boat in the distance. He was sailing in the opposite direction."

"Rik? You mean **Granny Angelica's** grandson?" said Tamera. "What could he be doing all the way out here?"

"I have no idea," said Chris, shaking his snout. "But I recognized his **YELLOW** shirt on the boat."

The **mouselets** sat up straight.

"A yellow shirt! Just like the sailor told us," Nicky said.

"Yeah . . ." replied Chris.

He quickly filled Tamera in on their conversation with the sailor at the Great Inagua PORT that morning.

Tamera was shocked. "Rik?! Do you really think he'd **sabotage** us?"

Her friend **shook** his snout. "I don't know . . . He could have been there for some other reason, but it's **suspicious**, don't you think?"

"You said that he was **SAILING** in the opposite direction from you," said Violet.

"So he was going **TOWARD** Little Inagua!"

Tamera frowned. "Rik wouldn't **HURT** a flea. He can be grouchier than a groundhog at times, that's true, but I don't think that he's **BAD** . . ."

The **mouselets** and Chris looked discouraged. They didn't know what to think.

CLUES!
SOMEONE SABOTAGED
THE GPS SYSTEM AND
THE RADIO ON TAMERA'S
BOAT, THEN SLASHED HER
RAFT . . . BUT WHO?

A NEW TEAMMATE

As Chris took the rudder, **guiding** the boat toward Little Inagua, the mouselets gazed out at the horizon. They were all thinking the same thing: Would this little island in the middle of the **Caribbean Sea** hold treasure or a trap? Their latest adventure, which had started out as a game, had turned into something a lot more real and a lot more **DANGEROUS**.

Tamera moved away from the side of the boat and checked the **map** again.

"Little Inagua must be the final stop on this voyage . . . I'm **sure** of it!" she whispered.

"Are you worried someone might have already found **Annabel's treasure**?" Colette asked.

Tamera shrugged. "It's possible, but Little Inagua is a perfect hiding place. The island is uninhabited. The only thing there is a **wildlife center**. And —"

She didn't get a chance to finish because Nicky shouted, "A **BOAT**! Look, there's someone on a boat over there. Whoever's on board is **signaling** us."

Chris gave the rudder to Paulina and joined his **friends** in the prow.

"She's signaling danger," the ratlet **cried**, alarmed.

"It's Kyla," Tamera replied, peering at the

Do you think it's still there?

It's a perfect hiding place!

boat through **binoculars**.

"What?" said Chris. "Let me see."

When Tamera passed him the binoculars, he nodded. "It's her, and her boat has **STOPPED**."

Tamera was consulting the sailboat's **GPS** and nautical maps.

"She must be stuck on the **shoals** . . . Look, that's what she's signaling now. She probably didn't realize how shallow it was here."

"Shoals?" asked Paulina. "What's that?"

"It's a part of the sea where the **WATER** isn't very deep. The sandy bottom is very close to the surface," Nicky explained. "It's **DANGEROUS** for sailboats because their hulls can get stuck and sometimes damaged."

"You mice stay here; I'll go over on the **RAFT** and bring back Kyla," Chris said.

It took only a few minutes to determine that Kyla's boat wasn't too damaged. But it couldn't sail until the tide changed. So Chris brought Kyla **BACK** to his own boat.

"Kyla!" Tamera said, **HUGGING** her. "Thank goodmouse we were *passing* by! Where were you going?"

The mouselet returned the hug. "I . . . I wanted to take a day **TRIP** in my boat, but I didn't notice the shoals . . ."

"It's *lucky* we saw you," exclaimed her friend. "We'll take you back to the port, but first you'll have to come with us to Little Inagua. Wait till I tell you our BIG news! You won't believe what we've discovered."

Tamera put her paw on her friend's shoulder. "Do you REMEMBER when I told you I'd found an old treasure **map**? Well, it's the real deal! First it led us to an island nearby, where we found a **clue** to our next destination: Little Inagua. We think we might find the TREASURE there."

"Really?" Kyla said.

"As long as we don't run into any other trouble," Chris added. He turned to Kyla. "Tamera didn't mention it, but someone's following us, and they're trying to **sabotage** us."

Kyla looked **startled**. "Wh-what? Do . . . do you know who it is?" she asked.

The ratlet shook his snout. "We don't know yet, but I bet we'll find out soon. It's hard to **hide** here on the open sea!"

"So do you want to come with us?" Tamera said. "We could take you home right away if you'd like . . ."

"Of course not," Kyla said quickly. "I want to come to Little Inagua with you. I'm starting to get swept up in this story, too!"

Chris and the mouselets shared a **LOOK**, and then smiled.

"**GREAT!**" said Tamera. "Then it's decided. Come on, gang, let's move those paws!"

TREASURE iSLAND

As Chris's boat approached Little Inagua, the **SUN** was slowly sinking, turning the sky **pink** and tossing fiery glimmers across the sea.

They reached the island in the raft — the coast was too **JAGGED** to make land in the sailboat. Chris secured the raft on a beach sheltered by a high, **ROCKY** wall, and the mouselets jumped out one by one.

The first to get her paws on the ground was Tamera. With one paw, she held the **map**; with the other, she shaded her eyes from the sun, studying the **STARK** landscape around them.

"What now? How do we know where to look for the **TREASURE**?" she asked, looking glummer than a gerbil without a wheel.

The Thea Sisters joined her. "Let's **explore**," suggested Violet. "Maybe we'll find a clue of some kind."

Chris and the mouselets walked toward the heart of the island, passing small bushes and cacti growing in the sand. As they scampered along, the sound of the waves died down, leaving only the sweet chirping of the BiRDS.

Suddenly, the mouselets heard something behind them — the sound of leaves moving and wings flapping. When they **turned**, they saw a flamingo with bright **PINK** feathers flying away to join its flock.

The **MOUSELETS** followed the bird's elegant **FLIGHT** across the sky until they saw it land on a dip in the landscape not far away.

"Mouselets," said Colette, pointing to the SPOT where the flamingo had landed, "let's go see what's over there. Think about it — one FLAMINGO led us here. Maybe another will take us to the treasure!"

They scurried toward a small sand dune. The **splendor** that greeted the mice at the top struck them all squeakless.

Below them was a small bay with gentle waves leaving streams of seawater here and there. But most extraordinary was the **beach**. It was covered with

BENEATH THE SAND

The mice stopped for a moment to *admire* this amazing sight.

"Flying fish sticks," murmured Pam, who couldn't drag her eyes away from the flamingos. "There are so many of them!"

"What an amazing discovery," breathed Tamera. "I had no idea there was such a large colony of FLAMINGOS on this island."

"Look," cried Nicky, pointing to a spot in front of them. "What are those smaller *grayish* flamingos?"

"Those are newborn babies," explained Tamera. "The color of their FEATHERS will change as they get older."

"Mouselets, let's try to get CLOSER so we can see better!" suggested Chris.

The Thea Sisters and Tamera agreed, but Kyla looked less than **enthusiastic**. "Aren't we here to look for TREASURE?"

Tamera took her by the paw. "We are, but this is a unique opportunity! We must observe this flamingo colony up close so we can **DESCRIBE** it to Professor Kendal."

Kyla had no choice. She followed everyone with a SIGH.

Carefully picking their way over the rocks, the eight mice headed down to the bay and soon found themselves on the beach.

The flamingos didn't seem concerned with the new arrivals, but they turned their LONG NECKS to observe the newcomers with a look that was part curiosity, part indifference.

A young bird stumbled up to Colette and

let out a raspy cry. When the mouselet took a step back, a bit timidly, Paulina started to laugh. "Hey, Coco, I bet it thinks you're one of its **parents**!"

Colette started to giggle. "How sweet!"

The sound of Chris's squeak interrupted her. "Mouselets, over here!"

The **THEA SISTERS** and Tamera joined their friend. Kyla trailed after them. She seemed a little impatient about this **DETOUR** from their treasure hunt.

"Look back there, at that rocky wall that

Oh, hi . . .

Wah! Wah!

DIVIDES the beach. There's a little cave," Chris said. "Most of the flamingos are in front of the entrance."

"*How funny*," said Pam. "They make very elegant guards."

As the mouselets drew closer, the flamingos turned to **see** them better. Then, all at once, they moved aside, leaving the entrance to the cave clear.

"**WEiRD!**" said Tamera. "Let's go see what's inside."

Inside, the cave was **VERY DARK**, and the mice went slowly to give their eyes time to adjust.

As soon as she could see clearly, Tamera noticed something strange. "Look at that little rock! There's a drawing of some kind on it . . ."

"It's a **FLAMINGO** carved into the

stone," cried Colette, tracing it with one paw. "Maybe it's a sign that the TREASURE is here!"

The friends GATHERED around the rock and started to examine the ground nearby, moving slowly AROUND the area.

Nicky started to dig in one corner. After a moment, she felt something smooth and cold under her pawtips. It was a rectangle made of metal.

It's a flamingo!

"Mouselets! Chris!" she shouted to her friends. "There's something here. Give me a paw with this!"

Everyone started to **DiG** in the sand.

When Tamera realized what the object was, she let out a squeak of joy. "It's a chest! An **old chest**!"

Soon they'd managed to pull an ancient-looking **wooden** treasure chest from the sand. They looked at it silently: A metal medallion inscribed with a big *A* covered the lock, which was now **corroded**.

With just a little force, the heavy lid opened.

Chris and the mouselets exchanged a brief, **INTENSE** look. Had they really **DISCOVERED** Annabel's treasure?

Holding her breath, Nicky slowly lifted the lid. The chest was filled with precious **gems** and gold coins! They sparkled in the rays of the setting sun.

"The TREASURE!" cried Tamera, her squeak cracking with emotion.

"We've found the pirate Annabel's treasure!"

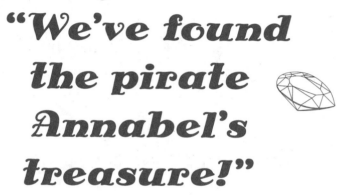

A LEGENDARY TREASURE

The mouselets and Chris dragged the **CHEST** out of the cave so they could take a better look at what was inside.

Kyla dug a paw into the TREASURE and brought it out. Her palm glittered with gold coins and pearls, rubies, emeralds, and sapphires. The precious **gems** glimmered extravagantly.

"Cheese and crackers!" cried Pam. "The treasure is real!"

"Yeah." Paulina nodded. "And it was here for all these YEARS, without anyone discovering it."

"I knew it!" Tamera cried happily. "This is so amazing!"

The mouselets were so caught up in the contents of the chest that they didn't realize someone had followed them and was drawing **CLOSER**.

"How are you, mouselets?" came a deep squeak from behind them.

The Thea Sisters and their friends were so $urpri$ed, they almost jumped out of their fur. When they turned around, they found themselves snout-to-snout with Rik. He had an **anxious** look on his snout.

"**YOU?!**" cried Chris. "What are you doing here?"

"I . . ." the ratlet

What are you doing here?

I followed you!

started to explain. "I **FOLLOWED** you . . ."

"I knew it!" Chris shouted. "You owe us an **explanation**!"

The ratlet wasn't expecting to be confronted like this. Looking confused, he took a few steps back. Then he stopped. "I was **AFRAID** that Tamera and her friends were in **DANGER**, so —"

Chris interrupted him. "Of course they're in danger, and you know all about it! I saw you sailing around the ISLAND where I found them trapped. Come on, confess: It was you who sabotaged their raft, wasn't it? Why did you do it?"

Rik's eyes widened. "Sabotaged?! Trapped?!" he cried. "Then I was right to suspect that something had happened!"

Sabotaged?!
Trapped?!

"There's no use making up some lie to cover your tracks! I know what you planned: You wanted to get your **paws** on the treasure!" shouted Chris.

Tamera and the **THEA SISTERS** gathered around the ratlets, who looked like they were about to break into a pawfight.

"Okay, everyone **CALM** down. Chris, let's give Rik a chance to explain," suggested Pam.

Rik **shook** his snout. "It's not me you need to look out for — it's her!" He turned in the direction where Kyla had been standing just a moment ago.

But she was gone — and the treasure chest was EMPTY!

THE UNEXPECTED TRUTH

Everyone looked around, **CONFUSED**. Where was Kyla?

"She's gone!" said Rik. "She fooled us all!"

"What are you saying?" exclaimed Chris. "How can you accuse her like that?"

"Don't you see? She's the reason I followed you!" Rik cried. "She's pulled the cheesecloth over all your eyes! Yesterday evening I ran into her as I was heading home. She didn't **see** me, but I heard her talking to someone on her phone. She said Tamera had discovered a treasure **map** and that *she* wanted to be the first rodent to find the treasure!

"At first I didn't pay much attention to what she'd said. But the more I thought about it, the more worried I got. So this morning I went out early to look for Tamera. I didn't find her at home, so . . ."

"You went to the PORT," said Paulina.

The ratlet nodded. "Yes. There wasn't anyone there, so I went back home again. Then I realized that Kyla's boat was missing, and I decided to go find her. When I saw you all heading to Little Inagua together, I thought I'd been worrying over nothing. But I decided to follow you, anyway, to warn you about Kyla."

"But where is she now?" asked Paulina in disbelief.

"Look over there!" cried Nicky, pointing to an outcropping on the nearest CLIFF. There was Kyla, almost at the top, her backpack full of coins and jewels.

"Bravo, you found the treasure!" she cried.

"Too bad you let me swipe it from right under your snouts! It was easier than taking cheese from a mouseling."

"Kyla, what are you doing?" Tamera cried in **disbelief**.

"Oh, don't start whining!" the other mouselet replied scornfully. "We both wanted the same thing: **Annabel's treasure!** Only I was a little sneakier . . . and a little smarter!"

It's too late!

"She took it all!" cried Colette. "She **emptied** the chest while you were arguing."

"That's right. Thanks to your **silly** bickering, I had a chance to take the treasure.

Now I'm going to sabotage your raft and **leave** on Rik's. By the time someone finds you, I'll already be far away . . ."

"Kyla," Chris tried to reason with her, "this treasure belongs to Inagua, not to you!"

"That's what you say!" she said. "It belongs to whoever finds it. See ya!"

Kyla turned and kept scrambling up the cliff. In her rush, she didn't notice she'd chosen the steepest path — a pile of rocks that dropped straight down to the sea.

Meanwhile, Nicky had taken advantage of Kyla's taunting to climb up behind her. The mouselet was so SWiFT and so athletic, she'd almost reached her. "Stop!" she shouted.

"YOU STOP!" replied Kyla. "I'm not going to lose the treasure now!" She kicked the ground, making sand fly into Nicky's eyes.

Nicky leaned back, TERRIFIED, and

slipped a few inches. Her friends screamed, but the mouselet held on by her pawnails.

The Thea Sisters sighed in RELIEF. Then they looked around frantically. What could they do to help their friend?

Colette spotted a FLAMINGO breaking off from the group and taking flight. It was heading straight for Kyla!

Frightened by the enormouse bird *flying* so close to her, Kyla took a step backward, lost her **BALANCE**, and wound up on the rocks very close to the edge of the cliff.

"Wha-what . . . ?" she could barely whisper. She scrabbled at the rocks, trying to get to safety.

Nicky noticed the dark, star-shaped **mark** on the flamingo. "BLACK STAR! IT'S YOU!" she cried, recognizing the animal she had LOVINGLY cared for at the **wildlife center**. "You came to defend me!"

The flamingo let out a sharp cry, as if agreeing, and then spread its wings and flew away.

Kyla stumbled, and the BACKPACK slipped off her shoulders and fell into the sea.

"Nooo!" the mouselet shouted, jumping after it and slipping down the cliff. By now she was dangling from the **ROCKS**, holding on with one paw. She was about to tumble into the water below.

"**Help!**" she cried, stifling a sob.

Everyone held their breath as Nicky used everything she knew about **ROCK CLIMBING** to inch her way closer to Kyla. When she was just a foot or two away, she **REACHED** out to the mouselet. "Come on, Kyla! Give me your paw!"

SURPRISED, the mouselet looked her in the eye. Her own eyes were filled with tears as she held out her paw. Nicky grabbed it and guided her to safety.

Together, the two mouselets climbed to the top of the **ROCKS**.

"Thanks," Kyla whispered, panting. "I don't **DESERVE** your help. I tricked you . . . I lost the treasure . . . and you still . . ."

Nicky smiled. "Who cares about the treasure? The important thing is . . .

we're

SAFE!"

THE BACKPACK'S BACK!

Kyla and Nicky slowly climbed back down from the rocks. The THEA SISTERS immediately threw their paws around Nicky.

"We were so afraid!" cried Paulina. "You shouldn't have CLIMBED all the way up there . . ."

"Just one wrong step and you'd have fallen into the sea!" Violet added with a shiver.

"It's lucky you're in such great shape," added Colette, drying a tear.

"RELAX, friends, I'm okay. Now we're all here, and — wait, not all of us. Where did Pam go?" asked Nicky, LOOKING around.

"I'm here, sisters!" exclaimed their friend, stepping out of the water. She was holding something big that was completely soaked.

"I can't believe it! You got the TREASURE back!" cried Tamera.

I couldn't leave it there!

"It fell into a shallow part of the water, and I figured I **couldn't** leave it there," Pam declared, squeezing her soaking wet pants. "The pirate Annabel would never have forgiven us!"

"You're AMAZING, Pam!" Nicky exclaimed.

Kyla took a swift step toward the BACKPACK and grabbed it, hugging it tightly.

The mouselets couldn't believe their eyes. Was it **POSSIBLE**, after everything that had happened, that Kyla still wanted to steal the treasure?

"Kyla, I don't think you should . . ." Tamera began, but she **STOPPED** when she saw that the mouselet was pawing the backpack full of jewels and coins to Chris.

"Today you all showed me many things," she said shyly. "That greed is dangerous . . . and that a team of **TRUE FRIENDS** is a treasure worth much more than jewels in an old chest."

Chris was squeakless for a moment. Then he **smiled**. "I'm happy you **understand** that. The treasure

Here. It's yours!

must return to Great Inagua."

"Annabel would have wanted that," murmured Tamera, watching the elegant trail of a flamingo across the sky.

"Now we can finally RETURN home," said Violet.

"First I must apologize to Rik," Chris began, clearing his throat. "I was . . . a bit . . . well . . ."

"Forget it!" The ratlet laughed. "The important thing is that we're all okay, and we can return to Great Inagua safe and sound."

Together, Colette, Nicky, Pam, Paulina, Violet, Tamera, Kyla, Chris, and Rik began walking along the path back to their boats.

As the Thea Sisters took a last look around, they breathed in the NATURAL beauty of Little Inagua, which was lit up with red REFLECTIONS from the last light of sunset.

"Do you hear that, mouselets?" Paulina said, cocking her ear toward the sea. "I can almost hear Ruby's squeak complaining about not applying for this study trip!"

"Just imagine what she'll say when she hears we found a pirate's TREASURE," Violet said, smiling.

"And that we carried it away in our paws!" Pam finished, laughing.

"This is definitely one of our most fabumouse adventures ever," said Colette, linking paws with her friends.

What an incredible day!

RETURN TO GREAT INAGUA

When they finally got back to Great Inagua, the **THEA SISTERS** were exhausted. The effort of their adventures had hit them all at once. The **mouselets** wanted nothing more than a nice long snooze.

Rik said good-bye and rushed back to his grandmother's to tell her the big news about the treasure. Kyla said good-bye, too, asking for forgiveness for her **BAD** behavior.

Chris and Tamera accompanied the Thea Sisters to the **cottage** where they were staying.

"What will we do with the treasure?" asked Colette as they scurried along. She glanced at the bulging **backpack** on Chris's shoulders.

"We'll give it to the authorities," the ratlet **explained**. "They'll decide what to do."

We'll give it to the authorities!

"I hope part of it can be donated to **OUR CENTER**," Tamera said. "It's the only way we can continue our research on the island's **animals**, and then you . . . you wouldn't have to leave."

When the mouselets reached their cottage, they turned to say good night to Chris and Tamera.

"Thanks, friends, for this **INCREDIBLE** adventure," said Nicky, smiling.

Chris and Tamera returned her smile. **"THANK YOU!** Especially for putting up with my stubbornness . . ." Tamera giggled.

Yawn!

"It was totally worth it! **Yawn!** Good night!" cried Violet. The others followed her inside.

Colette lingered by the window for a minute. She had a feeling something important was happening OUTSIDE.

"Coco, what are you doing?" Paulina whispered. "Are you **spying** on Chris and Tamera?"

"I'm not spying! I'm just . . . observing them, as a good **detective** of matters of the heart."

Pam and Nicky came and stood next to her. **Together**, the mouselets peeked out the window.

"Look carefully. **SEE** how close they are!" Colette said.

"Maybe that's because it's late and they don't want to squeak too loudly," suggested Nicky.

Colette ignored her. "I'm sure they're **declaring** their love!"

"You think? To me it looks like they're just saying good-bye," said Paulina. "What do you think, Violet?"

"**Zzzzzzz**" was her only response.

Her friends turned around. Violet had fallen **asleep** on the sofa!

"Classic. She's such a sleepysnout!" Paulina laughed.

Colette cheered and pointed to the scene outside the window. "Look! **I knew it!**"

Chris and Tamera were **hugging** each other tenderly.

The **mouselets** barely had enough time to move away from the window when Tamera

burst in, her eyes **shining**. "Mouselets, pardon the interruption — I know you're tired and want to go to bed, but I have some fabumouse news to share!"

"Really? What is it?" asked Colette **innocently**.

"After today's adventure, Chris and I finally found the courage to admit our tRue feeLiNgs. And we've just become engaged!"

We're engaged!

"Hooray!" cried the Thea Sisters.

Violet suddenly sat up. "What's happening? Is something wrong? Did someone steal the treasure?"

Everyone burst out laughing. "No, Vi, nothing like that . . . just good news!"

MERRYMAKING IN THE MOONLIGHT

A few days later, everyone was ready for the historical reenactment of the pirate Annabel's landing on Great Inagua.

Tamera could barely **CONTAIN** her excitement, especially because Chris was playing the part of James, the governor's son.

That **evening**, the whole town crammed into the harbor to witness Annabel's arrival. A light chattering rose from the crowd. As soon as the moonlight fell on the SHAPE of the pirate galleon, the chatter turned into an *ooooooh* of surprise.

Tamera, wearing Annabel's **coat**, climbed down from the galleon. Her pirate crew followed in her pawsteps. They were ready to attack the city.

When Tamera stepped in front of Chris, she tried to use a **harsh**, cruel tone, but Colette and the others heard a note of **sweetness** in her squeak as she "mousenapped" him.

At the end of the reenactment, the streets were filled with FESTIVITIES. Singing and dancing lasted late into the night.

Tamera scurried up to the Thea Sisters and hugged them. "Mouselets, I have GOOD NEWS to tell you: Inagua's authorities have decided to donate part of the treasure to our wildlife center!"

"Then the center will remain open?" asked Colette.

Tamera nodded. "ABSOLUTELY!

And Chris won't have to leave to find work!"
The **THEA SISTERS** gathered around Tamera and exchanged happy glances. They were remembering the beautiful beaches, the FLAMINGOS, their TREASURE hunt, and, more than anything else, the **friends** they had met on the way. It had been a marvemouse adventure!

Hooray!

What great news!

Don't miss any of these exciting Thea Sisters adventures!

Thea Stilton and the Dragon's Code

Thea Stilton and the Mountain of Fire

Thea Stilton and the Ghost of the Shipwreck

Thea Stilton and the Secret City

Thea Stilton and the Mystery in Paris

Thea Stilton and the Cherry Blossom Adventure

Thea Stilton and the Star Castaways

Thea Stilton: Big Trouble in the Big Apple

Thea Stilton and the Ice Treasure

Thea Stilton and the Secret of the Old Castle

Thea Stilton and the Blue Scarab Hunt

Thea Stilton and the Prince's Emerald

Thea Stilton and the Mystery on the Orient Express

Thea Stilton and the Dancing Shadows

Thea Stilton and the Legend of the Fire Flowers

Thea Stilton and the Spanish Dance Mission

Thea Stilton and the Journey to the Lion's Den

Thea Stilton and the Great Tulip Heist

Thea Stilton and the Chocolate Sabotage

Thea Stilton and the Missing Myth

Thea Stilton and the Lost Letters

Thea Stilton and the Tropical Treasure

Up Next!

Thea Stilton and the Hollywood Hoax

Be sure to read all my fabumouse adventures!

#1 Lost Treasure of the Emerald Eye

#2 The Curse of the Cheese Pyramid

#3 Cat and Mouse in a Haunted House

#4 I'm Too Fond of My Fur!

#5 Four Mice Deep in the Jungle

#6 Paws Off, Cheddarface!

#7 Red Pizzas for a Blue Count

#8 Attack of the Bandit Cats

#9 A Fabumouse Vacation for Geronimo

#10 All Because of a Cup of Coffee

#11 It's Halloween, You 'Fraidy Mouse!

#12 Merry Christmas, Geronimo!

#13 The Phantom of the Subway

#14 The Temple of the Ruby of Fire

#15 The Mona Mousa Code

#16 A Cheese-Colored Camper

#17 Watch Your Whiskers, Stilton!

#18 Shipwreck on the Pirate Islands

#19 My Name Is Stilton, Geronimo Stilton

#20 Surf's Up, Geronimo!

#21 The Wild, Wild West

#22 The Secret of Cacklefur Castle

A Christmas Tale

#23 Valentine's Day Disaster

#24 Field Trip to Niagara Falls

#25 The Search for Sunken Treasure

#26 The Mummy with No Name

#27 The Christmas Toy Factory

#28 Wedding Crasher

#29 Down and Out Down Under

#30 The Mouse Island Marathon

#31 The Mysterious Cheese Thief

Christmas Catastrophe

#32 Valley of the Giant Skeletons

#33 Geronimo and the Gold Medal Mystery

#34 Geronimo Stilton, Secret Agent

#35 A Very Merry Christmas

#36 Geronimo's Valentine

#37 The Race Across America

#38 A Fabumouse School Adventure

#39 Singing Sensation

#40 The Karate Mouse

#41 Mighty Mount Kilimanjaro

#42 The Peculiar Pumpkin Thief

#43 I'm Not a Supermouse!

#44 The Giant Diamond Robbery

#45 Save the White Whale!

#46 The Haunted Castle

#47 Run for the Hills, Geronimo!

#48 The Mystery in Venice

#49 The Way of the Samurai

#50 This Hotel Is Haunted!

#51 The Enormouse Pearl Heist

#52 Mouse in Space!

#53 Rumble in the Jungle

#54 Get into Gear, Stilton!

#55 The Golden Statue Plot

#56 Flight of the Red Bandit

Special Edition!

The Hunt for the Golden Book

#57 The Stinky Cheese Vacation

#58 The Super Chef Contest

#59 Welcome to Moldy Manor

Special Edition!

The Hunt for the Curious Cheese

#60 The Treasure of Easter Island

#61 Mouse House Hunter

#62 Mouse Overboard!

Special Edition!

The Hunt for the Secret Papyrus

Be sure to read all of our magical special edition adventures!

THE KINGDOM OF FANTASY

THE QUEST FOR PARADISE:
THE RETURN TO THE KINGDOM OF FANTASY

THE AMAZING VOYAGE:
THE THIRD ADVENTURE IN THE KINGDOM OF FANTASY

THE DRAGON PROPHECY:
THE FOURTH ADVENTURE IN THE KINGDOM OF FANTASY

THE VOLCANO OF FIRE:
THE FIFTH ADVENTURE IN THE KINGDOM OF FANTASY

THE SEARCH FOR TREASURE:
THE SIXTH ADVENTURE IN THE KINGDOM OF FANTASY

THE ENCHANTED CHARMS:
THE SEVENTH ADVENTURE IN THE KINGDOM OF FANTASY

THE PHOENIX OF DESTINY:
AN EPIC KINGDOM OF FANTASY ADVENTURE

THEA STILTON: THE JOURNEY TO ATLANTIS

THEA STILTON: THE SECRET OF THE FAIRIES

THEA STILTON: THE SECRET OF THE SNOW

THEA STILTON: THE CLOUD CASTLE

Meet
GERONIMO STILTONOOT

He is a cavemouse — Geronimo Stilton's
ancient ancestor! He runs the stone
newspaper in the prehistoric village
of Old Mouse City. From dealing with
dinosaurs to dodging meteorites,
his life in the Stone Age is full
of adventure!

#1 The Stone of Fire

#2 Watch Your Tail!

#3 Help, I'm in Hot Lava!

#4 The Fast and
the Frozen

#5 The Great Mouse
Race

#6 Don't Wake the
Dinosaur!

#7 I'm a Scaredy-Mouse!

#8 Surfing for Secrets

#9 Get the Scoop,
Geronimo!

#10 My Autosaurus
Will Win!

Join me and my friends as we travel through time in these very special editions!

THE JOURNEY THROUGH TIME

BACK IN TIME:
THE SECOND JOURNEY THROUGH TIME

THE RACE AGAINST TIME:
THE THIRD JOURNEY THROUGH TIME

MEET
GERONIMO STILTONIX

He is a spacemouse — the Geronimo Stilton of a parallel universe! He is captain of the spaceship *MouseStar 1*. While flying through the cosmos, he visits distant planets and meets crazy aliens. His adventures are out of this world!

#1 Alien Escape

#2 You're Mine, Captain!

#3 Ice Planet Adventure

#4 The Galactic Goal

#5 Rescue Rebellion

#6 The Underwater Planet

#7 Beware! Space Junk!

Meet
CREEPELLA VON CACKLEFUR

I, Geronimo Stilton, have a lot of mouse friends, but none as **spooky** as my friend CREEPELLA VON CACKLEFUR! She is an enchanting and MYSTERIOUS mouse with a pet bat named Bitewing. YIKES! I'm a real 'fraidy mouse, but even I think CREEPELLA and her family are AWFULLY fascinating. I can't wait for you to read all about CREEPELLA in these a-mouse-ly funny and **spectacularly spooky** tales!

#1 The Thirteen Ghosts

#2 Meet Me in Horrorwood

#3 Ghost Pirate Treasure

#4 Return of the Vampire

#5 Fright Night

#6 Ride for Your Life!

#7 A Suitcase Full of Ghosts

THANKS FOR READING, AND GOOD-BYE UNTIL OUR NEXT ADVENTURE!